Pride
and
Prejudice

Adapted by
Susanna Davidson

Illustrated by
Simona Bursi

Reading consultant: Alison Kelly
Roehampton University

Contents

This story is set nearly two hundred years ago, when life was very different, especially for women. At that time women did not have careers, and if, like the Bennet family in this story, they did not have much money, it was very important that they should marry — and marry well. Very few women had the luxury of marrying for love.

Chapter 1

The ball

The carriage was waiting; the night was warm. The Bennet sisters – Jane, Lizzy, Mary, Kitty and Lydia, were dressed in their finest ball gowns, flowers and ribbons threaded through their hair.

"Hurry, hurry!" cried their mother, urging them out of the house. "Kitty, do stop coughing. Oh, Jane! How beautiful you look. I'm so glad. It's so important you look your best tonight."

"And why is that?" asked her husband, Mr. Bennet, reluctantly leaving his study, a book still clasped in his hand.

"How can you be so tiresome?" retorted Mrs. Bennet, as they climbed into the carriage. "You must know what I mean. This ball is our first chance to meet Mr. Bingley! He has just moved to Netherfield Park. He is young and single and rich. Such a man *must* be in want of a wife."

"Perhaps he will choose you, my dear," said Mr. Bennet.

Mrs. Bennet laughed foolishly. "I was certainly pretty in my time. But now I only think of my daughters. If I could have one settled at Netherfield, and all the others well married, I'll have nothing to wish for."

"I can't think he will want to dance with any of them," replied Mr. Bennet. "They are all very silly girls, though Lizzy is slightly less silly than the rest of them."

"How can you say that about your own children?" cried Mrs. Bennet. "Ooh, you enjoy teasing me. You never think of my poor nerves."

"On the contrary, I know them well. They're my oldest friends. You've talked about them for twenty years."

Mrs. Bennet was about to protest when the carriage came to a halt. They had arrived at the ball.

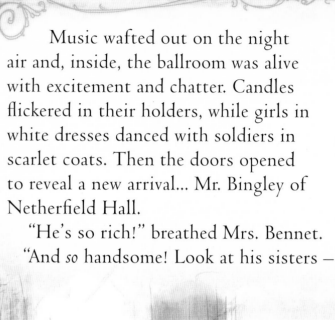

Music wafted out on the night air and, inside, the ballroom was alive with excitement and chatter. Candles flickered in their holders, while girls in white dresses danced with soldiers in scarlet coats. Then the doors opened to reveal a new arrival... Mr. Bingley of Netherfield Hall.

"He's so rich!" breathed Mrs. Bennet. "And *so* handsome! Look at his sisters –

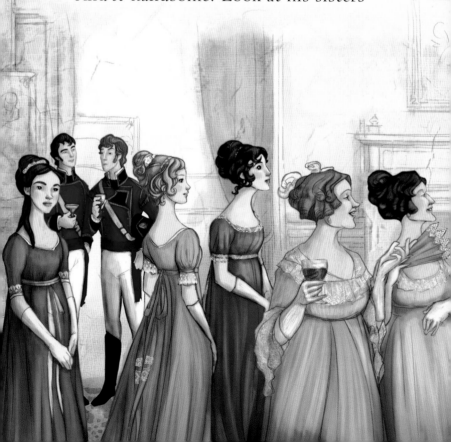

such elegant dresses."

"But have you heard?" cried her friend, Mrs. Lucas. "Mr. Bingley has brought his friend, Mr. Darcy, owner of Pemberley House. He is *even* richer."

"You talk of riches," said Mary, gravely, "but virtue is more important."

Lydia had already left the group. "Come on, Kitty!" she cried. "Let's go and flirt with the officers."

"Mr. Bingley's sisters look very proud and haughty," said Lizzy, observing them.

"They're not talking to anyone," Jane agreed, "but perhaps they're just shy."

"Oh, Jane, that's so like you to think the best of everyone. What about Mr. Bingley? Do you think him handsome?"

"Yes," sighed Jane, her eyes glowing.

A moment later, Mr. Bingley came up to them. He smiled at Jane. She smiled back. He asked her to dance.

From across the room, Mrs. Bennet looked on with great satisfaction.

Mr. Darcy, on the other hand, danced once with Jane, and spent the rest of the evening walking around the room with his nose in the air and his mouth turned down in a sneer.

"Come on, Darcy," said Mr. Bingley, leaving Jane's side for a moment. "I hate to see you standing by yourself in this stupid manner. Why don't you dance?"

Lizzy was at that moment without a dance partner, and was sitting on a bench at the side of the room, where she could overhear every word of Mr. Darcy's reply.

"You know I detest dancing, unless I know my partner particularly well. Besides, you are dancing with the only beautiful girl in the room."

"She *is* beautiful; you're right, but her sister's very pretty. Let me introduce you."

Mr. Darcy glanced at Lizzy. Catching her eye, he instantly withdrew his own. "She's passable, I suppose, but not pretty enough to tempt me," he said coldly. "I will not dance with a girl who has been rejected by other gentlemen."

Lizzy got up and walked away, allowing herself the pleasure of just one remark, which she made with her most enchanting smile. "Sir, you are all that is polite."

Leaving him swiftly, she went in search of her friend Charlotte Lucas, and eased her feelings by making a funny story of it.

"Poor Lizzy," comforted Charlotte. "To be only just passable! He has an excuse for being proud, perhaps. He has looks, an important family and fortune."

"Nonsense," snorted Mrs. Bennet,

overhearing their conversation. "I saw it all and I think he is a most disagreeable man. Another time, Lizzy, I would not dance with him even if he does ask you."

"I believe I can safely promise *never* to dance with Mr. Darcy," said Lizzy.

As Lizzy enjoyed watching those around her, she did not suspect that she was being watched – and by Mr. Darcy. Having first dismissed her, Darcy was now struck by her lovely dark eyes, her liveliness and wit.

"Well, Mr. Darcy?" whispered Bingley's sister, Caroline, in his ear. "Have you, like me, had enough? The noise. So vulgar! Jane Bennet is a sweet girl, but her family are really not our class, and their uncle is a shopkeeper. How low can you sink! You are quiet; what are you thinking of?"

"I'm thinking," Darcy replied, "what a fine pair of eyes I can see."

Miss Bingley at once fixed her gaze on his face. "Who do those eyes belong to?" she murmured softly.

His answer silenced her. "Miss Elizabeth Bennet."

Chapter 2

Love lost

Whenever the Bennets and Mr. Bingley now met, Mr. Bingley always sought out Jane. Lizzy could see that Jane was on her way to falling deeply in love with him.

She was surpised to find that Mr. Darcy always seemed to be watching her.

"I can't think why," she told her friend, Charlotte. "Unless he means to criticize me, for he never comes near me. But I like him too little to mind what he thinks of me."

Instead, her attention was caught by a new officer in town – a Mr. Wickham. Lydia was the first to meet him.

"Everyone is in love with him," she declared. "He's so handsome. If you come into town with me, I'll introduce you."

As soon as Lydia saw Wickham, she rushed over and dragged him back to meet her sisters, looking very pleased with herself.

Lizzy was immediately struck by his charm. His manners were so easy and engaging after Mr. Darcy's cold formality.

They fell behind the others and walked a little way together.

"Lydia says you often meet with the party at Netherfield," Wickham observed. "Do you know Mr. Darcy well?"

"As much as I ever wish to," said Lizzy.

"I have known him since I was a child. His father was the best of men and very fond of me. When he died, he left me a job as a clergyman. But when the position came up, Mr. Darcy refused to give it to me."

Lizzy gasped. "This is shocking! I thought him to be a proud, disagreeable man, but not as bad as this."

"I think he must have been jealous of me," said Wickham. "But the memory of his father means I wouldn't wish to tell people, and see Darcy disgraced in public."

Lizzy thought how good it was of Wickham to say so, and thought him all the handsomer as he said it. When they parted company, her head was full of him. She could think of nothing but Mr. Wickham, and what he had told her.

At home, Mrs. Bennet could hardly contain her excitement. "Mr. Bingley is holding a ball!" she told them. "It's for Jane, I'm sure of it!"

Lizzy planned to spend the evening dancing with Mr. Wickham, but when they arrived, he was nowhere to be found.

"I see how it is," she thought. "Mr. Darcy has made sure he isn't invited."

She turned, and found herself suddenly in front of Mr. Darcy. He asked her for the next dance, and took her so much by surprise that she agreed without knowing what she did.

They began the dance without speaking a word. As the silence went on, Lizzy began to suspect it would last the entire dance and was happy to keep it, until she imagined it might be a greater punishment for Mr. Darcy to talk.

"We must say something to each other, you know," she began. "It will look very odd otherwise. If I talk about the dance, you ought to make some remark about the size of the room."

He smiled, but said nothing.

At last, unable to stop herself, she said, "I recently met someone who knows you – Mr. George Wickham, who has just come to town."

The effect of his name was immediate. Mr. Darcy blushed and looked more haughty than ever.

Finally, he said, in a strained way, "Mr. Wickham has such happy manners, he makes friends wherever he goes. Whether or not he can *keep* them is another matter."

"He has been so unlucky as to lose your friendship," Lizzy remarked.

"He has," said Darcy. "And my good opinion once lost, is lost forever."

"I suppose you are very careful when you decide against someone?"

"I am," he replied.

The dance ended and they parted company, each feeling dissatisfied. For Lizzy the evening only got worse. She had to watch Lydia and Kitty flirting openly with the officers. Mary was playing the piano, very badly, and was refusing to stop. Worst of all was her mother telling everyone as loudly as she could how she would soon have a daughter at Netherfield. Lizzy saw Mr. Darcy watching her family with disdain, and wished him a thousand miles away.

The next morning, a letter arrived from Netherfield for Jane. She turned pale as she read it, and quickly left the room.

"What is it, Jane?" asked Lizzy, following her to their bedroom.

"It's from Caroline Bingley," replied Jane, in a quiet voice, her hand shaking slightly as she passed Lizzy the letter.

My dear friend,

We have left for London and I doubt we shall ever return to Netherfield. We are going to be spending much of our time with Mr. Darcy and his delightful sister, Georgiana. She and my brother have always been close and I hope, soon, that Miss Darcy and I shall be sisters...

"All this shows," said Lizzy, "is that Miss Bingley *means* her brother never to come back."

Jane smiled slightly, but shook her head. "She makes it very clear she doesn't want her brother to marry me. She means him to marry Darcy's sister."

"Of course he'll come back, Jane," said Lizzy. "I never saw a man more deeply in love than Bingley was with you."

But as the leaves turned and the chill of winter crept into the house, Bingley still didn't return. It pained Lizzy to see Jane's strained face, the sadness in her smile.

To make matters worse, their mother wondered daily when Bingley would come back. "I try to forget him," Jane told Lizzy, "and not to think of him, but it is so hard when mother speaks of him all the time. But I will forget him," she went on, "and be calm and contented as before."

Lizzy couldn't bear it for Jane any longer. She wrote to the Gardiners, her aunt and uncle in London, asking them to invite Jane to stay. They were the relatives she and Jane felt closest to. She could only hope that a change of scene would help Jane forget Mr. Bingley.

Chapter 3

A proposal

Home without Jane wasn't the same. Lizzy saw Wickham often, but he now spent most of his time with a rich young heiress, Mary King. Now that Darcy had left, it became known everywhere what he had done to Wickham. Everybody spoke of their affection for Wickham, and their dislike of Mr. Darcy.

Then another letter came, this time from her friend, Charlotte Lucas, who had recently married, inviting her to come and stay. Lizzy accepted with joy.

Charlotte's husband, Mr. Collins, was a vicar in Kent, living on the estate of Lady Catherine de Bourgh, whom he seemed to worship. He talked of nothing but Lady Catherine from morning until night.

"Her ladyship is wonderfully kind to us," Mr. Collins told her. "You are particularly lucky, Elizabeth, for she has invited us all to dine with her tomorrow."

Lizzy looked over, caught her friend's eye and had to try very hard not to laugh. "I look forward to it, Mr. Collins," she said.

The more Lizzy saw of Mr. Collins, the more she wondered why her friend had married him. He was a vain, pompous man.

"I see you are surprised by my choice of husband," said Charlotte, even though Lizzy had tried to hide it. "But I was never romantic, you know. I've only ever wanted a comfortable home. I'm not pretty like you, and would much rather have Mr. Collins than no one."

Lizzy said nothing. She felt deeply that she could never marry without love.

For the rest of that day, and the following morning, all Mr. Collins could talk of was their forthcoming dinner. As the weather was fine, they walked to Lady Catherine's grand house across a park. Servants ushered them into the drawing room and Lizzie gasped. Standing at the window, looking as proud as ever, was Mr. Darcy. She thought he started a little when he saw her.

"I have my nephews staying with me," said Lady Catherine, haughtily. "Mr. Darcy and Mr. Fitzwilliam."

"We have met before," said Mr. Darcy briefly, bowing at Lizzy, but making no effort to come over and talk to her.

Mr. Fitzwilliam, however, seemed delighted with Lizzy, and after dinner he drew her over to the piano, asking her to play as he turned the music.

"You are trying to frighten me, Mr. Darcy," said Lizzy, as he came over to watch her. "I know you have high standards."

"I can't believe you mean what you say," replied Darcy. "Of course I have no wish to alarm you."

"Do you know," Lizzy went on, addressing herself to Mr. Fitzwilliam, "I could tell you some very shocking things about Mr. Darcy."

"And what are those?" asked Darcy.

"The first time I met him, at a ball, he did not dance once. Even though there was more than one lady in want of a partner."

"Perhaps," said Mr. Darcy, "I should have asked, but I am not at ease with strangers."

"That is because you do not make the effort. I am not talented at playing the piano, but I have always supposed that to be my fault, for not trying harder."

Darcy smiled. "You are right. You have used your time better than me."

"What are you talking of?" interrupted Lady Catherine, ending the discussion. "Come over here where I can hear you."

The next morning, Lizzy was sitting by herself, writing to Jane, when to her great surprise, Mr. Darcy came in. He seemed just as astonished at finding her alone. They sat down, but after a few questions on either side, sank into silence.

He didn't stay long, but Charlotte couldn't believe he had come at all. "He must be in love with you, Lizzy," she said, but when Lizzy told her of his silence, she admitted it didn't seem possible.

Soon after Darcy's visit, Lizzy met Mr. Fitzwilliam on one of her walks in the countryside. He stopped when he saw her, and began walking along beside her.

"You're leaving soon?" Lizzy asked.

"Yes," Mr. Fitzwilliam replied. "If Darcy doesn't put it off again."

"And you must wait on him?" said Lizzy. "It seems he likes to have his own way."

"But so do we all, and he is very good to his friends. Only this summer, he saved his friend Bingley from a narrow escape."

"What do you mean?" asked Lizzy.

"Only that I heard Bingley was going to marry a very unsuitable girl and that Darcy managed to stop him."

Lizzy walked on, her heart swelling, unable to say anything. She got away as soon as she could and went straight to her room. *So Darcy was the cause of all Jane's unhappiness*, she thought. *He was the reason Mr. Bingley had gone so suddenly. He had ruined every hope of happiness for her sister...*

The others left for tea with Lady Catherine, but Lizzy couldn't go, claiming instead that she felt unwell.

She stayed in her room, re-reading Jane's letters, her anger growing as she was reminded of Jane's unhappiness.

The doorbell rang, and she went down to see who was calling. To her great amazement, Mr. Darcy was shown in. Hurriedly, he asked how she felt, then without a word, began pacing up and down.

Suddenly, he turned and spoke to her. "I have struggled, but it will not do. You must allow me to tell you how much I love and adore you."

Lizzy was too astonished to speak. Mr. Darcy seemed to take her silence as encouragement. "You are poor," he said. "Your family is nothing to mine. But I have tried not to love you and have found it impossible. Will you marry me?"

Lizzy tried to compose herself, but felt anger rise within her. "I cannot marry you," she said. "I'm sorry if this gives you pain, but I am sure it won't last."

Mr. Darcy struggled, paused, then spoke in a voice of forced calmness. "And this is your reply? This is all I deserve?"

"Had you asked me in a more gentleman-like way, I might have been more polite in my refusal. But I could never marry the man who has been so cruel to my sister. Can you deny that you separated Bingley from Jane?

Though your treatment of Wickham alone is enough to make me despise you."

"I am not ashamed of my actions," said Mr. Darcy. "And as for my proposal – can you expect me to be glad that you come from such a family?"

Lizzy felt herself growing more angry every moment. "You could not have asked me to marry you in any possible way that would have made me accept you," she said in a shaking voice. "From the moment I met you, I knew you were the last man in the world whom I would ever marry."

"And almost from the first, I loved you. You have said quite enough. I perfectly understand your feelings. Forgive me for taking up your time." With these words, he hurriedly left the room.

Lizzy felt weak, astonished. That Mr. Darcy should be in love with her, and for so long! That he wanted to marry her, in spite of all the objections! But his pride, what he had done to Jane, to Wickham... Lizzy heard the sound of the carriage. She knew the others were returning, and fled back to her room.

Chapter 4
The letter

Lizzy went straight out after breakfast, trying to clear her head with fresh air. She hadn't gone far along her usual walk when she saw Mr. Darcy ahead of her. She turned away, but he called her name, came after her and gave her a letter.

"Will you read this for me?" he asked.

Instinctively, she took it. Mr. Darcy gave a slight bow and walked away. Intrigued, Lizzy began to read...

Do not be alarmed, Miss Bennet. I am not going to repeat my offer of marriage. Yesterday, you accused me of two things. I only want the chance to defend myself.

It wasn't long before I realized Bingley was in love, but as I studied your sister, it did not seem to me that she loved him. And, as I watched your family at the Netherfield Ball, I became convinced that Bingley was about to become trapped in a marriage with an unsuitable family and a girl who did not love him. So I went with Bingley to London, where I told him that Jane did not return his affection. After that, it wasn't hard to persuade him never to return to Netherfield...

"How could he know Jane's true feelings?" thought Lizzy, still fuming. Though her face burned with shame when she remembered how her family had behaved that night. With shaking hands, she read on.

As for Mr. Wickham, he has not told you the whole truth. I offered him the job of clergyman, as my father requested in his will. Wickham turned it down. Instead, he asked for money to study law, which I gave him, but he frittered it away. Then, last summer, he tried to run away with my sister to force her to marry him — not because he loved her, but because he wanted her money.

If your dislike of me makes you doubt me, do ask my cousin, Mr. Fitzwilliam. I will only add,

God bless you.

Darcy

Lizzy didn't see either Darcy or Fitzwilliam before they left. By the time she was making her own journey home, she felt she knew Darcy's letter by heart.

How could she have been so wrong – she, who always prided herself on her insight? As her anger faded, she realized that Jane did hide her true feelings, even from those closest to her. She thought how she'd praised Wickham, been blinded by his charm...

At least she didn't have to face Wickham again. The officers had gone to Brighton. Lizzy was anxious to discover that Lydia had gone with them, in the company of one of her friends.

"Call her back, Papa," she begged. "She will only become more giddy and foolish away from home. And how Lydia acts affects us all... how we are all judged."

Mr. Bennet laughed. "Do you mean to say Lydia is frightening away husbands for you and Jane? Don't make yourself uneasy, my love. Wherever you and Jane go, you will be respected and valued."

Lizzy had to leave it at that. She was glad she had one thing to look forward to – a trip with her aunt and uncle, the Gardiners.

"We have decided to go to Derbyshire," her aunt wrote.

Instantly, Lizzy thought of Pemberley – Mr. Darcy's home. "But surely," she thought, "I can go to Derbyshire without seeing him?"

The trip was delayed once, twice, until at last, they set out, Lizzy longing to see new sights.

Chapter 5

Pemberley

After a few weeks they came to a town where Lizzy's aunt had spent her summers as a child. "We are not far from Pemberley," said Mrs. Gardiner. "I've heard it's a very impressive house. Don't you want to see it Lizzy?"

Lizzy thought of the embarrassment of seeing Darcy again, but the innkeeper where they were staying assured her that the family was away. So to Pemberley they went.

They approached Pemberley through a large park. The driveway wound through woods and then, at the top of a hill, Lizzy had her first view of the house. It stood on the opposite side of a valley, above a winding river and gently sloping banks. Lizzy was delighted. She had never seen a more beautiful spot. *And to think, I could have been mistress of all this...*

A housekeeper showed them the lofty, elegant rooms, filled with fine furniture.

"This place could have been my home..." thought Lizzy, in wonder.

They passed a portrait of Mr. Darcy, hanging above the stairs.

"And this is your master?" asked Mrs. Gardiner.

"Yes, and I know none so handsome," said the housekeeper, proudly. "He's a good

master. I haven't had a cross word from him in all my life."

Lizzy longed to hear more. She turned back to look at the portrait, smiling down at her. In that moment, she felt gentler towards him. She thought of his love for her and remembered its warmth, rather than the way he expressed it.

They walked out across the lawn and, to
her astonishment, there he was, twenty yards
in front of her. Their eyes met, they both
blushed. He started, then came towards
her. He spoke politely, and Lizzy listened,
amazed at the change in him.

He, too, seemed ill at ease. He asked her
the same question twice, as if his thoughts
were distracted. Then he recollected himself
and asked to be introduced to her aunt and
uncle, greeting them warmly.

"I thought you weren't coming until tomorrow," said Lizzy, desperate to let him know she hadn't pursued him here.

"We came early," he said. "My sister is here too, just arrived. Will you come inside? She is eager to meet you."

His sister's eagerness, Lizzy thought, must depend on what Darcy had told her. *Did he still love her then, after all she had said to him?*

Over the next few days, they saw each other frequently. Darcy invited them to dinner, and he and his sister made morning calls to the inn where they were staying.

Mr. and Mrs. Gardiner watched and wondered. It was clear to them when they saw Darcy that he was very much in love, but they could not guess Lizzy's feelings.

On the fourth day, a letter arrived from Jane.

Dearest Lizzy,

We have just had bad news.

Lydia has left Brighton, and run away with Mr. Wickham. They have been traced as far as London and it doesn't seem as if they have any plans to marry. Our father has gone to London to see if he can find them.

Do return. We need our uncle's help at this terrible time.

Jane

Lizzy started up, about to run out of the door in search of her uncle, when Mr. Darcy came in. He saw her pale face and shaking hands. "What is it?" he cried at once. "What is the matter?"

Lizzy couldn't answer him, tears poured down her face. Darcy sent a servant out to fetch the Gardiners. Then he waited until Lizzy could speak.

"I can't hide the truth," she said. "Lydia, my youngest sister, has run away with Mr. Wickham to London. And to think I knew what he was like, but kept it a secret. If only I had said... How will they ever be found?"

Darcy said nothing, he only walked up and down the room, frowning.

Watching him, Lizzy thought how all his love for her must have vanished in that moment. How could he want to marry her, knowing her family's shameful secret? And now that she had no power over him, she realized for the first time, how much she had grown to love him.

Chapter 6

Love & marriage

At home, she found her mother continually crying upstairs, and her father a changed man. "I should have listened to you, Lizzy," he said. "You begged me to bring Lydia home again."

"Don't be too hard on yourself," Lizzy said. "They may yet be found."

"Well, your uncle is in London, looking for them, but I don't hold out much hope. Wickham will never marry her. She's too poor for him. And then she'll be ruined."

A week later, Jane and Lizzy were walking in the garden, when Kitty came running from the house. "A letter!" she cried. "A letter has come from Uncle Gardiner. Lydia and Wickham are to be married!"

They found their father in the orchard. "Your uncle must have given Wickham a great deal of money to marry her. I don't know how I shall ever repay him."

Mrs. Bennet leaped from her bed at the news, the shame of Lydia's actions instantly forgotten. "My dear, dear Lydia. To be married – at sixteen! How delightful."

When Lydia arrived home, arm in arm
with her husband, she was the same Lydia
– wild, noisy, unashamed. "You must all
congratulate me," she said to her sisters, "for
I am married and you are not, even though *I*
am the youngest."

"I am not sure we like your way of getting
husbands," said Lizzy.

"But it was such fun!" said Lydia. "Even
though the Gardiners looked so stern at our
wedding, just like Darcy–"

"Darcy?" cried Lizzy.

Lydia clapped her hand over her mouth.
"Oh! I wasn't meant to tell you. He was
there. He arranged it all!"

Lizzy felt her heart racing. *Mr. Darcy had gone to town, searched for Lydia, saved her from ruin! Had he done it for her?* She felt humbled at the thought, but knew she must think of him no more.

Lydia and Wickham left for the north, where Wickham was to join a new regiment. Mrs. Bennet declared she felt flat now that Lydia had gone, until she heard the news that Mr. Bingley was coming back to Netherfield...

"It means nothing," said Jane. "I shall be able to meet him with perfect calmness."

A few days later, he called.

"Look," cried Kitty, watching him from the window. "He's brought his friend with him. That tall, proud man none of us liked."

Lizzy buried her head in her book. Jane looked a little paler than usual.

Bingley entered, both embarrassed and pleased, and went immediately to Jane's side. Darcy barely spoke, and Lizzy saw he was once again proud and silent.

Could I expect it to be otherwise! thought Lizzy. *Yet why did he come?*

As soon as they had gone, Lizzy and Jane walked out together.

"I am glad the first meeting is over," Jane said. "Now when we meet it will be only as acquaintances."

"Oh Jane, take care," laughed Lizzy. "I think you are in danger of making him as much in love with you as ever."

Bingley came again on Tuesday, and took his usual seat by Jane.

Mrs. Bennet could not be more excited, continually plotting to leave Bingley and Jane alone together. At last, the moment arrived. He called, alone, Mr. Darcy having gone to town. One by one, Mrs. Bennet swept her other daughters from the room.

When Lizzy returned, Jane's face was aglow with smiles. "Oh! It's too much!" she cried. "Why can't everybody be this happy? We are to be married."

Lizzy was delighted.

"I congratulate you both," said Mr. Bennet, as the rest of the family joined them. "You are perfectly suited."

Mrs. Bennet could talk of nothing else. "Five thousand pounds a year!" she cried. Lydia and Wickham were forgotten. Jane was her very best child.

"Can you believe it?" said Jane, that night. "When he went to town last year, he really loved me, and only the persuasion that I didn't love him, kept him away. If I could only see you as happy, Lizzy."

A week after Bingley's proposal, the family was sitting in the drawing-room when a carriage was heard on the driveway. It was Lady Catherine de Bourgh. They were all astonished.

Lady Catherine stalked into the room and looked around dismissively. "I wish to speak to Elizabeth," she declared. "You may walk with me on that prettyish little lawn you call a garden."

Lizzy went with her, unable to think what she might have to say, unless perhaps she had brought a message from Charlotte.

"You know, of course, why I have come?" said Lady Catherine.

"I do not," replied Lizzy honestly.

"Do not trifle with me, Miss Bennet!" replied Lady Catherine in an angry tone. "I have heard alarming news – that *you* are soon to be married to my nephew, Darcy. It cannot be true. Tell me it is not true."

Lizzy felt flustered, confused. She didn't know where the story had come from, but most of all, she felt anger at her ladyship's tone. "You may ask questions. I may choose not to answer them," she replied.

"Miss Bennet, do you know who I am? You cannot marry him. You are of no importance in this world."

"He is a gentleman, I am a gentleman's daughter. So far, we are equal."

"But who is your mother's family? Who are your uncles and aunts? Will you promise me never to marry him?"

"I will make no such promise. You have just insulted me in every possible way."

Lady Catherine swept herself off to her carriage. "I shall make sure this marriage never happens," she called out. "I am most seriously displeased."

Lizzy watched her go, her heart fluttering with anger. She knew Lady Catherine would go straight to Darcy. If he had been wondering before what to do, surely now he would decide never to propose again.

But when Bingley came again to visit them, he brought Darcy with him. They set out on a walk together, Bingley falling behind with Jane, until it was just Darcy, Lizzy and Kitty. And then Kitty left them, to visit her friend, and Lizzy bravely went on alone with him.

She seized her moment. "I have been wanting to thank you, for what you did for Lydia," she began.

He turned, obviously surprised that she knew. "I did it thinking of you," he said.

There was an uncomfortable pause. "If you still feel as you did last April," Darcy went on in a rush, "tell me so at once. *My* affections and wishes are unchanged."

Lizzy turned to him then, and told him as well as she could, how much her feelings had changed. Darcy's face flushed with happiness.

They walked on, without knowing in what direction. Lizzy learned she had Lady Catherine to thank for Darcy's return.

"I knew that if you did not love me, you would be frank enough to tell her," said Darcy. "What she told me gave me hope. When I proposed before I said unforgivable things. I was proud..."

"Let's not think of it," said Lizzy. "Neither of us behaved well. You must have hated me after that evening."

"At first I was angry, but only at myself. I tried to show you at Pemberley how I had changed."

By the time they arrived home it was dark. Darcy went straight to Mr. Bennet, while Lizzy sought out her mother.

"Ten thousand pounds a year!" she cried, all her former dislike of Darcy vanishing in an instant. Lizzy could only be relieved that Mr. Darcy was not around to hear it.

After Darcy had left, Mr. Bennet called Lizzy to him. "I gave my consent at once," he told her. "He is not the sort of man you refuse. But do you really love him? He is rich, but I thought you despised him."